For Phil and our 'wee ones' – Sean, Bethany, Joey and Katy. And for Mum and Dad. Love you all. S.W.
To Heather and Tony, with love and thanks. C.J.

OXFORD
UNIVERSITY PRESS

Great Clarendon Street, Oxford OX2 6DP

Oxford University Press is a department of the University of Oxford.
It furthers the University's objective of excellence in research, scholarship,
and education by publishing worldwide in

Oxford   New York

Auckland   Cape Town   Dar es Salaam   Hong Kong   Karachi
Kuala Lumpur   Madrid   Melbourne   Mexico City   Nairobi
New Delhi   Shanghai   Taipei   Toronto

With offices in

Argentina   Austria   Brazil   Chile   Czech Republic   France   Greece
Guatemala   Hungary   Italy   Japan   Poland   Portugal   Singapore
South Korea   Switzerland   Thailand   Turkey   Ukraine   Vietnam

Oxford is a registered trade mark of Oxford University Press
in the UK and in certain other countries

British Library Cataloguing in Publication Data available

ISBN: 978-0-19-272919-4 (paperback)

3 5 7 9 10 8 6 4 2

Printed in China

Paper used in the production of this book is a natural, recyclable product made
from wood grown in sustainable forests. The manufacturing process conforms to the
environmental regulations of the country of origin

Wee William

Sheryl Webster and Cecilia Johansson

OXFORD
UNIVERSITY PRESS

Wee William was the smallest in his family.
Everything about him was small.

'Your tiny squeak,'
said Martha.

'Your teeny ears,'
said Daddy.

'And your little wriggle,'
said Mummy.

When Mummy took William to
feed the ducks she asked him,
'Now, William, do you need to go?'
before they left the mousehole.

But William said, 'No.'
So off they went.

William carried his piece of bread, very carefully, all the way to the pond.

He followed Mummy across the stepping stones,

remembering to miss out the wobbly one.

But then William
gave a little wriggle.

'Mummy,' he said.
'I need a wee — NOW.'

'Don't worry,' said Mummy.
'We can feed the ducks
another time.'

And feeding the ducks turned
into finding somewhere
for William to go.

That evening William was very excited:
he was going to watch Martha in the
Mouse Pantomime. Mummy, Daddy,
and William took their places.

The light faded and the chorus began to sing.
When he saw Martha on the stage William
began to wriggle. Mummy knew what this
meant and guided William quietly to the back.

'Mummy,' he whispered. 'I need a wee — QUICK!'
'I know,' said Mummy, 'just slip behind the cowslips.'
'But everyone will see,' William worried.
'No they won't,' hushed Mummy.

By the time they got back to their seats,
the show was over.

The next day was Friday
and that meant . . .
swimming at Puddle Pool!

But as soon as William
was in the water . . .

he called, 'Daddy! I need a wee.'

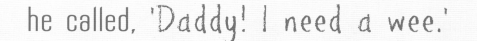

Daddy lifted William out of
the pool and they made it
to the nearest bush . . .
by a whisker.

When William came back from his dip, Mummy said,
'Let's go and pick some berries for dinner.'

William loved the way Mummy juggled the berries and balanced them on her nose.

He giggled and giggled so much that he started to wriggle.

'Are we nearly home, Mummy? I need a wee.'

They weren't nearly home but luckily
they were just passing Mrs Twitch's burrow.

Mrs Twitch knew exactly
where William needed to go.
'Straight ahead and down
the first tunnel,'
she said, 'it's not far!'

'Thank you,'
said Mummy.

After dinner William and Martha went to play hide-and-squeak
with Prickle and Gulliver on Buttercup Brow.

William hid first, and tried
to keep very still behind
his stone . . .

but he seemed to be waiting for an awfully long time . . .

And finally when Gulliver
shouted, 'Found you!'
there was a little puddle
by William's feet.

Close to tears, William scurried home as fast as his legs would carry him.

That night Mummy cuddled William.
'Don't be sad about today,' she said.

'Everyone has little accidents.
But if you remember to wee
before you do things . . . then
you won't worry about needing
to wee *while* you do them.'

And she gave him
a gentle squeeze.

The next morning Mummy and Daddy had
a surprise for William and Martha.
They were going to the Woodland Fair!

Before they left the mousehole, Mummy asked,
'Now, William, do you need to go?'
And this time William said, 'Yes!'

William spun . . .

and bounced . . .

and see-sawed . . .

without a single
wriggle.

After lunch Daddy took William to go behind the clover patch.
Then he was ready for one last ride — the Bumpy Leaf Slide.

'Will you come with me,
Mummy?' said William.
Mummy smiled. She picked up
their leaf and they dragged it
to the start of the ride.

William was ready.
Mummy wasn't so sure.
It was a very long way down.

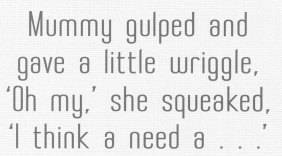

Mummy gulped and
gave a little wriggle,
'Oh my,' she squeaked,
'I think a need a . . .'

all the way
to the end of
the slide.